W9-AWX-955

This book belongs to:

_____

A first baby bear.

A second baby bear.

You're All My Favorites

Sam McBratney

illustrated by Anita Jeram

CANDLEWICK PRESS
CAMBRIDGE, MASSACHUSETTS

Once upon a time

there was a mother bear,

a father bear,

and three baby bears.

And a third baby bear.

Whoever tucked them in at night
always said the same thing to them:
"You are the most wonderful baby bears
in the whole wide world!"

One night, after Mommy Bear
had tucked them in, and after she had said,
"You are the most wonderful baby bears
in the whole wide world,"
the baby bears began to wonder.

"But how do you know?" they asked their mommy bear. "How do you know we are the most wonderful baby bears in the whole wide world?"

"Because your daddy told me,"
said Mommy Bear.
"When your daddy saw you on the night
you were born, he said—
and I remember it very well—he said,
'Those are the nicest baby bears
I have ever seen.
They are the nicest baby bears
anyone has ever seen!' "

That was a good answer.

The three baby bears snuggled

down as content as could be.

But one day, the first baby bear
began to think. He wondered if the
other two bears were nicer than he was.
They had patches, after all,
and he did not. Maybe his mommy
really really liked patches.

And the second baby bear began to wonder.
Maybe Daddy loves the other two
more than me, she thought.
They were boy bears, after all,
and she was not.

And the third baby bear

began to worry.

I'm only the littlest, he thought.

Everybody's bigger than me!

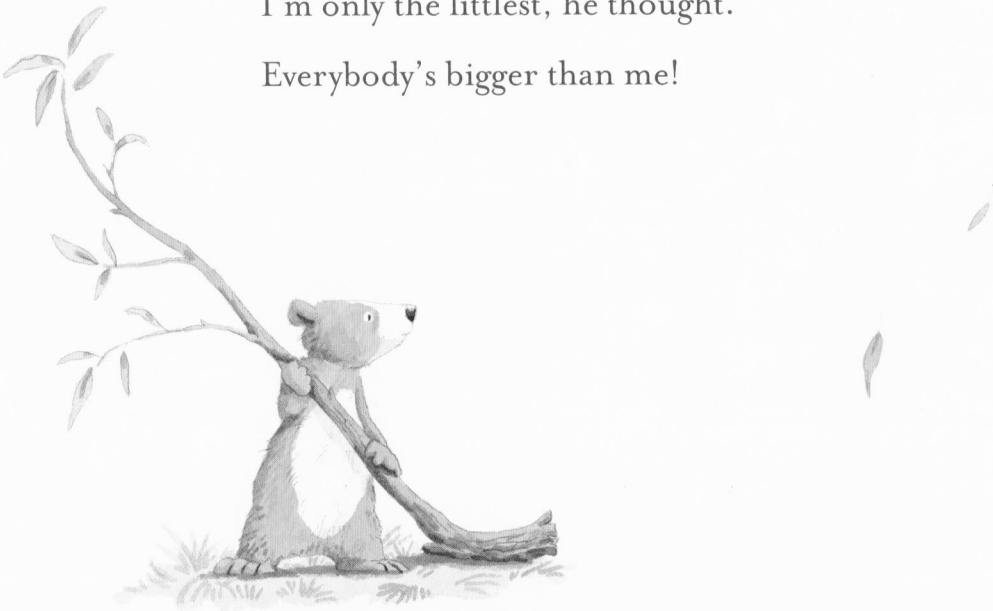

So that night the three baby bears asked their daddy bear,

"Which one of us do you like most?

Who is your favorite?

We can't all be the best."

"Yes, you can," said Daddy Bear. "I know you can because I heard your mommy say so. When she saw you" — and Daddy Bear picked up the first baby bear to give him a cuddle — "she said, 'That is the most perfect first baby bear that anyone has ever seen.'"

"Even with no patches?"

"Patches don't matter at all," replied his daddy, as he tucked him in.

"And when your mommy saw you" —Daddy Bear picked up the second baby bear— "she said, 'That is the most perfect second baby bear that anyone has ever seen.' "

"Even if I'm not a boy?"

"Girl or boy, it makes no difference," said her daddy, and he hugged her tight.

"And when your mommy saw you" — Daddy Bear
lifted the last baby bear into his arms—
"she said, 'That is the most perfect third
baby bear that anyone has ever seen.'"
"Even if I'm the littlest?"
"Biggly or littley,
we love you just the same.
So there. Three favorites.
You're all my favorites!"

And the best baby bears in the whole wide world
went to sleep as happily as could be, because
that was a good answer, too.

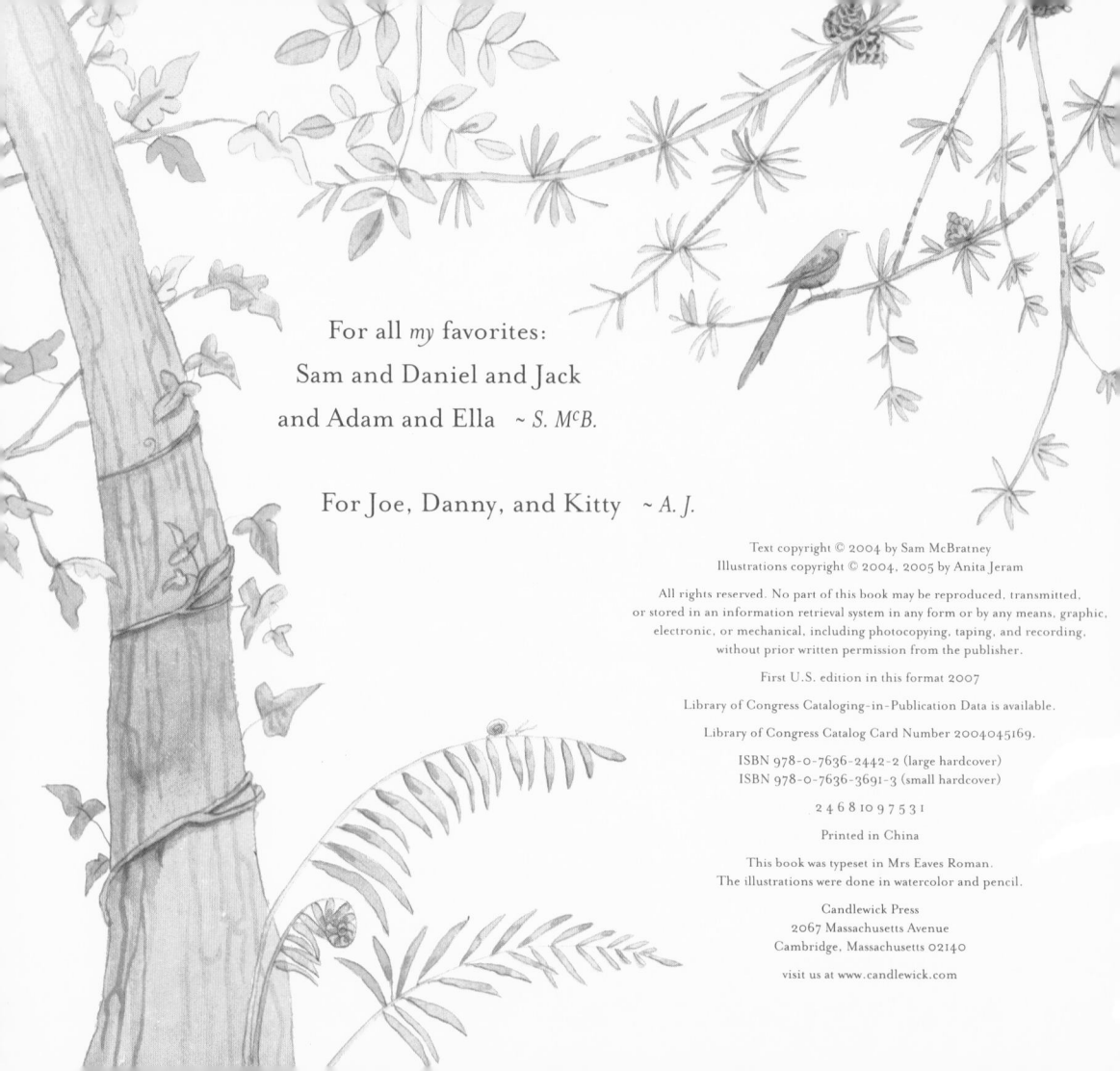

For all *my* favorites:
Sam and Daniel and Jack
and Adam and Ella ~ *S. McB.*

For Joe, Danny, and Kitty ~ *A. J.*

Text copyright © 2004 by Sam McBratney
Illustrations copyright © 2004, 2005 by Anita Jeram

All rights reserved. No part of this book may be reproduced, transmitted, or stored in an information retrieval system in any form or by any means, graphic, electronic, or mechanical, including photocopying, taping, and recording, without prior written permission from the publisher.

First U.S. edition in this format 2007

Library of Congress Cataloging-in-Publication Data is available.

Library of Congress Catalog Card Number 2004045169.

ISBN 978-0-7636-2442-2 (large hardcover)
ISBN 978-0-7636-3691-3 (small hardcover)

2 4 6 8 10 9 7 5 3 1

Printed in China

This book was typeset in Mrs Eaves Roman.
The illustrations were done in watercolor and pencil.

Candlewick Press
2067 Massachusetts Avenue
Cambridge, Massachusetts 02140

visit us at www.candlewick.com